In memory of my father
–J. L.

For Beth de Jarnette,
librarian extraordinaire
–J. E. D.

SIMON & SCHUSTER BOOKS FOR YOUNG READERS
An imprint of Simon & Schuster Children's Publishing Division
1230 Avenue of the Americas, New York, New York 10020
Text copyright © 2005 by John Lithgow
Illustrations copyright © 2005 by Jack E. Davis
All rights reserved, including the right of reproduction in whole or in part in any form.
SIMON & SCHUSTER BOOKS FOR YOUNG READERS is a trademark of Simon & Schuster, Inc.
Book design by Dan Potash
The text for this book is set in Fink Roman.
The illustrations for this book are rendered in colored pencil, acrylic, dye, and ink.
Manufactured in China
4 6 8 10 9 7 5
Library of Congress Cataloging-in-Publication Data
Lithgow, John, 1945–
Marsupial Sue presents "The Runaway Pancake" / John Lithgow ; illustrated by Jack E. Davis.– 1st ed.
p. cm.
Summary: Sue, a kangaroo, and some of her Australian animal friends put on a play called "The Runaway Pancake."
ISBN-13: 978-0-689-87847-3
ISBN-10: 0-689-87847-8 (hardcover)
[1. Theater–Fiction. 2. Animals–Australia–Fiction.] I. Davis, Jack E., ill. II. Title.
PZ7.L6977Mar 2005
[E]–dc22
2004010990
0313 SCP

# MARSUPIAL SUE

### Presents

## The Runaway Pancake

John Lithgow

Illustrated by Jack E. Davis

Simon & Schuster Books for Young Readers

New York   London   Toronto   Sydney

Marsupial Sue presents
THE RUNAWAY PANCAKE

Cast
(in order of appearance)

Narrator . . . . . . . . . Adelaide Rabbit
Auntie May . . . . . . . . Marsupial Sue
Old Dog Tray . . . Bartholomew Koala
Cow . . . . . . . . . . . . Sydney Wombat
Donkey . . . . . . . . . Winifred Wallaby
Wolf . . . . . . . . . . . . . Perth Platypus
Bear . . . . . . . . . . Melbourne Sheep
Fox . . . Neville, the Tasmanian Devil

Stage Manager . . . . . . Collie Dundee

Runaway Pancake designed and
operated by Team Bandicoot

This is the story of the Runaway Pancake. It begins with Auntie May, who decided to cook a pancake for her lunch one day. She went to her pantry and took out everything she needed to make a big, round pancake. She took out flour and eggs, butter and milk. She mixed the ingredients in a big bowl, poured the batter into a patty-cake pan, and put the pan into a hot oven.

Now, children, listen care-
fully. You must never, ever,
EVER cook a pancake in a
hot oven. And my story will
tell you why.

While her pancake cooked, Auntie May did her household chores. She
dusted, she swept, and she vacuumed the living room. When she turned
off her vacuum cleaner, she heard a muffled sound in her kitchen. It
was coming from her oven. It sounded like this: "Hey! Hey! Lemme outta
here! Lemme OUTTA here!!"

Auntie May gripped the handle of the oven door, opened it just thiiiiiiis much, and . . . BANG! Out jumped the Runaway Pancake!

The Runaway Pancake had two eyes, a nose, and a mouth. He wore a naughty expression on his face. He rolled across the kitchen floor, across the living room floor, out the front door, across the front yard, out the front gate, and off down the road. Auntie May chased after him, shouting, "Come back! Come back! You're my LUNCH!"

The Runaway Pancake answered her with a little song. He sang,

"No, no.
No, no, no.
I'm too fast, you're too slow.
Pan, pan, patty-cake pan,
I can get away from you, I can!"

And he rolled along, rolled along with Auntie May chasing after him. Pretty soon he came to an Old Dog named Tray, lying by the road and chewing on a bone. Old Dog Tray looked up at the Pancake and said, "Mmmmm. Pancakes go good with bones. You're going to be my lunch."

And the Pancake sang,

"No, no.
No, no, no.
I'm too fast, you're too slow.
Pan, pan, patty-cake pan,
I got away from Auntie May,
I can get away from you, I can!"

And he rolled along, rolled along with Auntie May and Old Dog Tray chasing after him. Pretty soon he came to a Cow standing in a hay field, chewing on her cud. The Cow looked at the Pancake and said, "Mmmoooooooo. Pancakes go good with cud. You're going to be my lunch."

And the Pancake sang,

"No, no.
No, no, no.
I'm too fast, you're too slow.
Pan, pan, patty-cake pan,
I got away from Auntie May,
I got away from Old Dog Tray,
I can get away from you, I can!"

And he rolled along, rolled along with Auntie May, Old Dog Tray, and now the Cow chasing after him. Pretty soon he came to a Donkey in the tall, green grass. The Donkey looked at the Pancake and brayed out, "Hee-haw! Hee-haw! Pancakes go good with grass. You're going to be my lunch."

And the Pancake sang,

"No, no.
No, no, no.
I'm too fast, you're too slow.
Pan, pan, patty-cake pan,
I got away from Auntie May,
I got away from Old Dog Tray,
I got away from the Cow in the hay,
I can get away from you, I can!"

And he rolled along, rolled along with Auntie May, Old Dog Tray, the Cow, and now the Donkey chasing after him. Pretty soon he came to an old, gray Wolf. The Wolf looked at the Pancake, licked his chops, and said, "Smack, smack. Pancakes go good with chops. You're going to be my lunch."

And what did the Pancake say?

"No, no.
No, no, no.
I'm too fast, you're too slow.
Pan, pan, patty-cake pan,
I got away from Auntie May,
I got away from Old Dog Tray,
I got away from the Cow in the hay,
I got away from the Donkey's bray,
I can get away from you, I can!"

And he rolled along, rolled along with Auntie May, Old Dog Tray, the Cow, the Donkey, and now the Wolf chasing after him. Pretty soon he came to a big, brown Bear, sitting by a honeybee hive, licking honey off his big, brown paws. The Bear looked at the Pancake and said, "Grrrrrrrr. Pancakes go good with honey. You're going to be my lunch."

He was right about the honey, but he was wrong about the lunch. Because the Pancake sang,

"No, no.
No, no, no.
I'm too fast, you're too slow.
Pan, pan, patty-cake pan,
I got away from Auntie May,
I got away from Old Dog Tray,
I got away from the Cow in the hay,
I got away from the Donkey's bray,
I got away from the Wolf all gray,
I can get away from you, I can!"

And he rolled along, rolled along with Auntie May, Old Dog Tray, the Cow, the Donkey, the Wolf, and now the Bear chasing after him.

He rolled along, rolled along.

Pretty soon he came to a big hill.

He started to roll up the hill. Pretty soon he came to a big oak tree beside the road.

And lying in the shade of that big oak tree, taking it easy on that hot afternoon, was the sly, old, red . . .

Fox.

The Pancake rolled to a stop and caught his breath. He looked at the Fox, and the Fox eyeballed the Pancake. Then the Fox smiled and said, "You're. Going to be. My. Lunch."

The Pancake threw back his head, laughed heartily, and sang,

"No, no.
No, no, no.
I'm too fast, you're too slow.
Pan, pan, patty-cake pan,
I got away from Auntie May,
I got away from Old Dog Tray,
I got away from the Cow in the hay,
I got away from the Donkey's bray,
I got away from the Wolf all gray,
Even got away from a Bear today,
I can get away from you, I can."

And the Fox said, "I beg your pardon?"

Once again, the Pancake sang,

"No, no.
No, no, no.
I'm too fast, you're too slow . . ."

"I'm sorry, Pancake," interrupted the Fox. "As you may
know, foxes are a trifle hard of hearing. Perhaps if you
roll a little closer and sing a little louder, I might better
grasp your meaning."

And the Pancake rolled to within one yard of the Fox's
snout, and a little louder he sang,

"No, no!
No, no, no!
I'm too fast! You're too . . ."

"I'm sorry, Pancake dear," said the Fox. "I still can't hear you. If you roll a little closer and sing a little louder, I might better decipher your declamation."

So the Pancake rolled to within one foot of the Fox's snout, and even louder he sang,

## "NO, NO.
## NO, NO, NO.
## I'M TOO FAST, YOU'RE . . ."

"I'm sorry, Pancake darling," said the Fox. "I still can't hear you. If you roll a little closer and sing a little louder, I might better apprehend your expostulation."

So the Pancake rolled to within ONE INCH of the Fox's snout! And as loud as he could he sang,

"NO, NO!

The Fox ate the Pancake with one enormous gulp. And you'd think that was the end of the story, wouldn't you?

Well, it isn't. Because the Fox looked up, and what do you think he saw? He saw Auntie May, Old Dog Tray, the Cow, the Donkey, the Wolf, and the Bear standing over him, hungry and tired and panting and sweating in the hot afternoon sun.

They were so angry at the Fox for eating their lunch that they chased
him out of the forest, and he was never seen or heard from again.
And you'd think THAT was the end of the story, wouldn't you?

Well, it isn't. Because if you listened closely to the Fox's tummy, you could still hear the Runaway Pancake (because the Fox had swallowed him whole, you see). The Pancake was still singing his song, but it sounded different now. It was a sad and slow song, not nearly so cocky, not nearly so arrogant. The words were different too. This time the Pancake sang,

"Dear, dear.
Dear, dear, dear.
I am eaten up, I fear.
I ran and I ran as fast as can be.
I got away from Auntie May,
I got away from Old Dog Tray,
I got away from the Cow in the hay,
I got away from the Donkey's bray,
I got away from the Wolf all gray,
Even got away from a Bear today.
But that sly old Fox
Was the end of me."

And you'd think THAT was the
end of the story, wouldn't you?

Well, it is.